GYMNASTICS
COMEBACK

Selina Li Bi

Raintree is an imprint of Capstone Global Library Limited, a company incorporated in
England and Wales having its registered office at 264 Banbury Road, Oxford, OX2 7DY –
Registered company number: 6695582

www.raintree.co.uk
myorders@raintree.co.uk

Designed by Dina Her
Original illustrations © Capstone Global Library Limited 2021
Originated by Capstone Global Library Ltd

Image Credits
Shutterstock: Brocreative, (grunge) design element, cluckva, design element, Eky Studio,
(stripes) design element, Polhansen, (beam) design element, sportpoint, Cover

978 1 3982 0424 9

British Library Cataloguing in Publication Data
A full catalogue record for this book is available from the British Library.

Every effort has been made to contact copyright holders of material reproduced in this book.
Any omissions will be rectified in subsequent printings if notice is given to the publisher.

Printed and bound in the United Kingdom

CONTENTS

CHAPTER I

DAYDREAMER

Suzy stretched her arms and shoulders. Her body tensed as she watched her teammate Mina launch off the vault. Mina flipped through the air in her purple leotard before nailing the landing.

Suzy inhaled sharply. She was about to perform her routine. *Can I do it as perfectly as Mina did?* she wondered.

Coach Pat's voice echoed across the gym. "Mina, remember to push through those shoulders!" she shouted.

The chatter around the gym turned to soft whispers. Another teammate walked across the beam. Her toes dipped down and brushed the side of the beam. She paused and pivoted on the balls of her feet.

All the girls except Suzy wore matching green scrunchies in their ponytails. This only made Suzy feel worse.

Suzy felt out of place on her new team. It was only her second day of practice, but she wondered if she'd ever fit in with the older girls.

Suzy held her breath. Suddenly she felt as if everyone was watching her.

You can do this, Suzy told herself. *Just pretend you are back at club gymnastics.* She smoothed back the wisps of her long, black hair that had escaped her tight bun.

She moved to the corner of the blue mat and struck a pose, one hand reaching up and the other at her waist. Suzy imagined Beethoven's Fifth

Symphony playing. It was her mum's favourite. Suzy had carefully selected the piece to go with her floor routine.

She hoped to surprise her mum with it at her first meet – if her mum showed up. She rarely did these days, and Suzy wasn't sure why.

Suzy launched into her routine, hips swaying to the right, then to the left.

Gymnastics made Suzy feel alive. Whether she was performing dance moves on the mat or a front-tuck dismount off the beam, she loved the feeling of tumbling through the air. She felt strong and fierce. Plus, she enjoyed the challenge of trying new moves.

She raced down the mat, gaining momentum for her first tumbling pass, and felt the familiar rush of adrenaline. She bounced off the mat and both legs sailed through the air. She pushed through her shoulders and twisted her hips. Moving into a front tuck, she somersaulted mid-air and stuck the landing. Her arms darted up and out in a finishing pose.

If only she could capture this moment and keep it in a jar.

"Nice! You nailed that landing," said Katie, a senior and the Ravens' team captain. She stood near the uneven bars, dusting her hands with chalk.

Suzy smiled. "Thanks."

Katie was the top gymnast at North High. She was also a former club gymnast. Suzy knew her from the club, but Katie was several years older. Katie made everything look easy – straight legs, pointed toes and secure landings.

Suzy watched Katie practise on the uneven bars. Katie leapt off the springboard and grasped the low bar. Her toes shot up towards the ceiling, her blonde ponytail whipping side to side as she circled the bar. She swung to the high bar, circled again, then released. Her body flipped through the air with ease.

Katie stuck the landing and Suzy clapped for her, along with some of their other teammates. Suzy couldn't help feeling as if she'd never be as good as Katie.

I need to practise more, Suzy thought. She walked back to the mat she'd been practising on and charged across it again. She launched into a cartwheel followed by a front tuck, her body somersaulting through the air. She stuck the landing again.

Rebecca, another top gymnast, gave her a high five. "Your floor routine is great," she said, tightening her scrunchie. "We have a good chance against South, thanks to you. The Panthers are our biggest rivals. It's been going on for years."

Suzy swallowed hard. "I'll do my best!" she said eagerly.

Suzy's combination of tumbling skills and graceful dance moves had made her unbeatable in club gymnastics. It was the reason she'd earned a place on the senior school team.

Last spring, Coach Pat had watched her perform a double back tuck at a club competition, a new trick she had just learnt.

"You're tough," Coach Pat had said. "You did well performing a difficult move. You ought to try out for our senior school team."

At try-outs last week, Suzy had learnt that one of the seniors who had graduated last school year, Dana, had dominated the floor event. Now the team would be counting on Suzy to take Dana's place in competition.

Suzy thought about club gymnastics as she walked to the water fountain. She had been a member since she was eight years old. But this autumn would be different. Competing at senior level meant more pressure to perform. So far, the senior school team didn't feel as comfortable as Suzy's club team, where she knew the other girls so well.

Just then, Coach Pat walked over. "Bravo," she said to Suzy. "You show a lot of promise. We're really glad you're on the team. Keep up the great work."

"Thanks, Coach," Suzy said.

A former national gymnast, Coach Pat was petite and muscular. She had a reputation for being tough, but Suzy had always liked being pushed to perform her best.

Coach Pat turned towards the gym. "Hey girls, gather round and listen up," she called in a booming voice.

The team huddled together near Coach.

"Our big meet against South is two weeks away. I expect all of you to work hard, eat well and get lots of rest leading up to the competition," Coach Pat said. "And I can already tell that Suzy here is going to nail that floor routine."

All heads turned towards Suzy as she felt the heat rise to her cheeks. She tried to ignore the stares of her teammates.

"Right, Coach," she replied, but she didn't believe it. She had the other events to think about as well – the vault, the uneven bars and the beam.

* * *

After practice, Suzy rode her bike home from school. She pedalled fast, thinking about how hard she would have to work over the next couple of weeks to perfect her floor routine and improve on the other three events.

"Slow down!" someone shouted.

Suzy stopped pedalling and glanced back. It was her best friend, Tiffany. Her face was red from trying to catch up.

"Hiya! What's up?" Suzy said.

"I've just come out of book club," said Tiffany as she rode alongside Suzy. "How's practice going? I knew you'd make the senior team. You're so good." She smiled, her braces twinkling in the sunlight.

"Are you nervous?"

"Are you kidding? I'm freaking out," said Suzy. "Everyone is so good. But it's only been a couple of days. I'm still getting used to Coach Pat and the team."

"I'd be freaking out too," said Tiffany. "I couldn't do a split if my life depended on it." She giggled. "I'll stick to my books. Shakespeare is less demanding."

"Not sure about that," said Suzy. She thought about all the homework she had to do when she got home. The autumn piano recital was the week after the big competition, and having had gymnastics try-outs last week, Suzy hadn't practised at all. She knew her mum would be on her case.

Gymnastics was all Suzy really wanted to do. Her team was counting on her, and she would need to practise hard to get her routine just right before their first competition.

If only Mum understood, she thought as she pedalled. She felt the pressure build up like a balloon ready to pop.

In her mind, she added a new trick to her floor routine. Pushing off the mat, her knees bent, she accelerated into a backwards rotation and landed securely on both feet.

But can I pull this off in competition? Suzy wondered.

What if she didn't stick the landing? What if she fell during one of her tumbling passes? What if she messed up a dance move?

One mistake and she'd be letting the whole team down.

Her heart thumped just thinking about it. Her mind started to spin out of control.

What if . . . What if . . .

"Stop!" Tiffany shouted.

Suzy immediately clutched the brakes on her bicycle and tried to swerve towards the shoulder of the road, but she lost her balance.

In front of her, a pick-up truck slammed on its brakes. She heard a horn honk as her bike skidded out from under her.

CHAPTER 2

SIGNS

Suzy found herself on the pavement, her bike lying beside her. Her whole body trembled, but it was her wrist that hurt the most.

"Watch where you're going!" the driver of the truck yelled.

Tiffany ran to Suzy's side, her eyes wide. "Are you okay?"

Suzy shook her head. As she tried to move, the sharp pain in her wrist shot up her arm. She immediately thought of gymnastics and groaned.

Her tears came fast, thick streams falling down her cheeks.

"What am I going to do?" she said, shoulders heaving.

* * *

Suzy woke to the sound of voices nearby – Tiffany's in particular. "I don't know. It happened so fast."

Suzy's wrist throbbed with a sharp pain, reminding her of her fall.

Mum's concerned voice followed. "She's been so busy between gymnastics and piano and schoolwork. And now this. It's all too much."

After the fall, Tiffany had helped Suzy get home. Because Suzy's mum wasn't home from work yet, Tiffany had got an ice pack from the freezer and helped Suzy get settled on the sofa. Suzy had dozed off while icing her wrist.

"It was an accident, Mrs Lee. It could've been worse," Tiffany said.

"She's lucky," Mum replied.

A sizzling noise came from the kitchen. The sweet scent of jasmine rice mixed with another salty aroma drifted past Suzy.

Mum's probably making stir-fried vegetables, Suzy thought.

She popped up from the sofa. "I can hear you two talking about me. Not cool."

A moment later, Mum came to her side. Suzy had been hoping for a plate of food. Instead, Mum held a familiar octagonal jar in one hand. It was Tiger Balm, a healing ointment.

"How are you doing?" said Mum. "I've got something to put on your wrist."

"It had better work. I need to heal fast so I can practise," said Suzy.

Mum smiled. "And play the piano."

"I know," Suzy said with frustration. "The recital

is coming up, but so is my first senior gymnastics competition."

"Maybe you should give gymnastics some more thought. You haven't been able to practise your piano. And now this," replied Mum.

"I fell off my bike," said Suzy. "This has nothing to do with gymnastics."

Suzy stared at the leaping tiger on the label of the Tiger Balm jar. She'd had a few minor injuries during club gymnastics, but nothing like this.

"You're right. Let's focus on getting you better." Mum twisted off the cap and spread the ointment on Suzy's wrist. "I'm going to take you to a doctor – straight after we've eaten dinner."

"Yeah," said Tiffany, "I think that's a good idea."

Just then Suzy's younger brother, Andy, walked in. His dark, spiked hair stuck up in all directions. "What's going on? I smell Tiger Balm. Is Suzy hurt again?"

"Mind your own business, Andy," Suzy said.

Her mum frowned at her.

"What happened?" asked Andy.

"I hurt my wrist. I'm afraid I won't be ready for our first meet in two weeks." Suzy's voice cracked.

She thought of Coach Pat and her teammates. She wanted to cry. Why did this have to happen now, at the beginning of her first senior season?

"The girls on the team are going to be so disappointed," said Suzy. "What am I going to do?"

"It'll be okay," said Tiffany. "You'll be back soon. I've got a good spy novel you can read in the meantime."

"Hope you didn't break it," said Andy.

Suzy shot Andy a dirty look. "You're not helping."

"You both need to stop," Mum said. She looked at Suzy. "Let's eat. Then we need to go to the doctor to get this looked at."

* * *

White, sterile walls surrounded Suzy and her mum at the clinic. Fluorescent lights hummed like a drone of bees. Suzy's wrist ached. It was swollen and bruised. *What if the injury is serious?* she thought.

"Everything will be all right," Mum said, chewing on her pinky fingernail. Suzy could tell her mum was worried. This could be bad.

Dr Wong walked into the room wearing a white lab coat, her dark hair pulled back in a bun. "What have we here?" she said.

Suzy looked down. She didn't want to know what was wrong with her wrist. She wanted to rewind time. *Please, please let it be nothing,* she thought. *I have to practise, and I have to compete. Everyone is counting on me, even if Mum doesn't understand.*

"My daughter is a lucky girl," Mum replied. "She could have been hit by a car."

"Oh no!" Dr Wong said. "What happened?"

"I was riding my bike and crashed," Suzy said. She felt her mother's stare. "And I landed on my wrist."

"Let's take a look," said Dr Wong. "Can you move it at all?"

"Sort of." Suzy gently moved her wrist. She touched the spot where it was sore and swollen.

Dr Wong examined Suzy's wrist and jotted down notes in the file. "By the amount of movement you still have," she said, "I think it's a very mild sprain. Ice it every three to four hours for the next couple of days."

"When can I go back to gymnastics practice?" asked Suzy.

"I'd give it a week and see how you feel," said Dr Wong.

"And what about her piano?" Mum asked.

Dr Wong winked. "Can't forget about that. Again, see how you feel. In the meantime, I'll fit you with this soft brace to protect your wrist. After about four days, you can remove it."

Suzy winced as Dr Wong put the brace on her arm.

"If there's no pain after four days, I'd like you to do some stretches," Dr Wong said. "You'll want to bend your wrist forwards, holding for five seconds, then backwards, doing several sets." She handed Suzy a sheet of paper with instructions. "Take it easy now."

* * *

On the ride home from the clinic, Mum didn't say a word. Suzy wanted to break the silence, but her stomach ached with worry.

"I wish you'd consider trying another sport. Gymnastics takes up so much time. You haven't been able to keep up with piano and homework," Mum finally said.

"I have to do this," said Suzy.

"You don't *have* to do anything." Mum's brows narrowed.

"I love gymnastics." Suzy paused. "You're cross with me."

"I'm not," replied Mum.

"Then why do you have that crease between your brows?"

Mum's face softened. "I don't like seeing you hurt. Promise me you'll take it easy."

"I promise," said Suzy. "The doctor said I could practise on my wrist in a week."

"She said to see how you feel," said Mum. "And don't forget about the piano recital. You need to practise for that too."

Suzy nodded as if she agreed, but she really only cared about getting back to gymnastics. She thought about all the new tricks she wanted to try. She imagined herself flying through the air, moving from a round-off to a back handspring followed by a full twist.

Don't give up, she told herself.

CHAPTER 3

PRESSURE

The next day, Suzy dreaded going to practice.
In her last period, personal development, she could
hardly focus.

*What are my teammates going to say when they find
out about my injury?* she wondered. *How will Coach Pat
react?*

When the last bell rang, Suzy went to the locker
room and changed into her leotard. Even though
Dr Wong had told her not to practise for a week, she
decided she could at least do some stretches. Maybe

nobody would notice. Maybe she could hide her injury for now. She took off the wrist brace and stuffed it into her backpack.

As she walked into the gym, Suzy thought about her teammates from club gymnastics. She missed them. And she missed the old gym too. This gym was smaller and darker. It didn't smell nice and the equipment was older. But as she watched the Ravens leap and spin through the air with confidence, she realized how lucky she was to be on this team.

Suzy stretched her arms and shoulders, aware of her sore wrist the whole time. She stretched out her hamstrings, then moved to the mat. Swaying her hips, she tried to go through the motions of her floor routine, avoiding the tumbling passes.

Rebecca hung from the high bar, doing windscreen wipers with her legs. Her bright-green leotard glistened. A few minutes later she circled the bar, her auburn ponytail swaying, toes pointed, body straight and aligned.

Suzy sighed. She wished she could be swinging off the uneven bars, tumbling in the air, doing backflips. She attempted a leap in mid-air, but her left arm tightened, sending pain down to her wrist. As her feet touched the floor, she winced.

On the opposite side of the gym, Katie balanced on the beam. She looked like a flamingo, standing on one long, thin leg. She grasped the other leg, her toes almost over her head. She lowered her leg, then cartwheeled across the beam. Her feet bounced off the beam and she flipped backwards, body straight as she sailed through the air before landing on the mat. She smiled as if she was in competition.

"Good work," said Coach Pat. "Remember to keep your legs glued together."

Suzy paced the mat, rubbing her wrist. It throbbed, making her wince again.

"Suzy, what's going on? Do you need to see the trainer?" Coach Pat's voice beckoned from the side of the gym. "Come over here."

Suzy dashed over.

"What did you do to your wrist?" asked Coach Pat.

Suzy felt frozen. There was no use trying to hide the injury any longer. "It's just a sprain."

A few girls stopped what they were doing and stared.

Suzy's face grew warm. "The doctor said I could practise in a week," she said quietly.

Katie stepped closer, still out of breath from tumbling. She locked eyes with Suzy. "What the heck, girl?" Her face scrunched, her gaze moving to Suzy's wrist.

"What happened?" asked Coach Pat. "It looks swollen."

"I fell off my bike," mumbled Suzy.

"Perfect timing. Just before our big meet," Katie said as she rolled her eyes.

Suzy wanted to crawl into a hole and hide.

"Sometimes sprains are worse than breaks," said Coach Pat.

"The doctor said I'd be better in a week," Suzy repeated.

"I expect you to stay conditioned," said Coach Pat. "Wall sits. One-arm push-ups. Work on your leaps and jumps. Visualise your routines."

"Yes, Coach," said Suzy.

Coach Pat started to walk away. She stopped, her jaw jutting forwards. "And one more thing. Stay focused."

Suzy swallowed. "OK, Coach." She bit into her bottom lip. She wanted to practise like everyone else. Leaps and wall sits weren't going to cut it if she wanted to nail her floor routine against the Panthers.

Katie was now halfway across the gym, jumping off the springboard and landing hands-first on the vault and pushing off into a handspring with a half twist in mid-air before landing with both feet sinking into the mat.

Suzy felt a pinch of jealousy. Walking towards the wall, the room spun. What if her wrist didn't get better before the big meet? What if she didn't have enough time to practise?

With her back against the wall, Suzy stood, her feet hip-width apart. She slid her back down the wall until her knees were at a 90-degree angle. She held herself in a seated position as long as she could, arms out straight in front of her. Her wrist ached. She probably should have kept the brace on for more support. Suzy watched the clock on the wall, holding the position for a minute.

Across the gym, near the uneven bars, a cloud of chalk dust hung in the air. On the high bar, Rebecca performed a giant, rotating 360 degrees, her body fully extended.

"More power!" shouted Coach Pat.

Rebecca's feet began to descend. She swung around the bar again, legs together, body straight. Then she released the bar, her body tumbling through the air. She landed steadily, with only one foot taking a tiny step forwards.

They all look so good, thought Suzy. On the mat, she moved into a straddle stretch, extending her arms over to the right, then to the left. Her wrist throbbed as she stretched. She wanted to be back to normal. *Breathe,* she told herself. One week. She could handle it.

CHAPTER 4

DUMPLINGS

After practice, Suzy sat at home at the kitchen table and followed the doctor's instructions. She iced her wrist and thought about what Coach Pat had said. *Visualise your routines.* Suzy imagined herself on the mat, moving into a split, her body in perfect alignment. After holding it for a few seconds, she stood gracefully and spun round.

Her mind paused and she switched to the vault. She visualised herself running full speed and launching off the springboard. She pushed off the vault with both hands and moved into a somersault, landing in a finishing pose.

Suzy sighed. Visualising her routines was certainly not the same as actually practising them.

After icing her wrist, Suzy smeared on the Tiger Balm, the strong smell of menthol rising up her nostrils. It was only day two, but she pulled out the stretching instructions. *Bend the wrist forwards and hold for five seconds.* It seemed so simple. Maybe if she got a head start, she'd heal faster. She gritted her teeth and stretched her wrist forwards. It was sore, and a mild pain ran up her arm. She stopped, her palms sweating.

Suzy took a tub of leftover fried rice out of the fridge. She got a fork and took a bite. Even though she was injured, practice had been a grind. The swarm of emotions drained her, but she had to keep focused. She took a sip from her water bottle and thought about her floor routine. She closed her eyes and imagined herself on the mat again. The music picked up speed, and Suzy raced down the mat, heart thumping. Her body took flight with a round-off. Her feet hit the mat briefly, then she arched her body backwards and rotated through the air.

Mum walked in before Suzy could visualise herself sticking the landing.

"I bought ingredients to make dumplings," said Mum. She was carrying a couple of bags of groceries. "I could use some help."

Normally, Suzy would be thrilled. She loved her mum's dumplings and she liked making them too. But she was stressed. "Do we have to?" she finally said.

"I thought you'd be excited." Mum looked puzzled. "Is your wrist bothering you?"

It wasn't her wrist that bothered her most. It was the fact that she couldn't practise her routines and she couldn't try new tricks.

"My wrist is okay," said Suzy, putting the brace back on.

"I see you've been looking at the instructions from Dr Wong," said Mum. "Remember, she said to do those stretches *after* your brace is off."

Suzy's back tightened and her wrist ached. "I know," she replied. "I was just curious."

"Make sure you rest and take it slowly. You don't want to reinjure it," said Mum.

Suzy helped Mum prepare the dumplings. After an hour, the kitchen worktop was covered with bits of chopped food. Suzy put the package of wonton wrappers and a bowl of ground pork in the middle of the worktop. The pork was mixed with chopped scallions, ginger, garlic, water chestnuts, sesame oil and soy sauce. Mum cracked an egg and separated the egg white into a small dish.

"You look tired. Shame you can't play the piano. I hope you get better before the recital," Mum said.

"And the big meet," replied Suzy. Her shoulders tightened thinking about the homework she needed to finish and the English essay she had to write.

Gymnastics did take up a lot of time, but the last thing on her mind was the piano recital.

Suzy dipped her index finger into the egg white and spread it along the edge of the wonton wrapper. Then she placed a dollop of meat in the middle and folded the wrapper over like a blanket. The egg white was sticky like glue. She pinched the edges of the wonton wrapper into a half-moon shape.

She felt clumsy with her wrist brace, just like she had felt at gymnastics practice. It was going to take a lot of energy to stay in shape and strengthen her wrist. Again her mind wandered to the upcoming competition. She didn't have long to build up her strength.

Then the words tumbled out of her mouth. "Are you coming to my first senior school meet? It's in two weeks." She thought about the music she had picked for her floor routine and how much she wanted to surprise her mum.

"I don't know. Let's see if you can compete first," said Mum.

"Trust me. I'll be competing," Suzy said.

"I'd hate to see you disappointed," replied Mum. "It takes time to heal, and I'd rather hear you play the piano. You hardly practise."

"Mum, stop," said Suzy.

Andy marched in. "Yeah. Why do you do gymnastics anyway?" He reached for a wonton wrapper. "Seems like you're always stressed."

Suzy threw Andy a nasty glare. "Why don't you help instead of bothering me?" she asked.

His voice shifted to a higher tone, an imitating whine. "Why did this have to happen to me? Poor me . . . My wrist hurts. . . . Doesn't sound like fun. Maybe you *should* just play the piano."

Andy's words stung. Her brother had a way of telling the awful truth. Gymnastics did sometimes stress her out. She never seemed to have enough time to finish anything.

"But you're tough. You'll make a comeback," said Andy.

Suzy felt a little better hearing that. She knew she couldn't let the team down. *I'm tough enough to get over this injury,* she told herself.

Mum started frying the dumplings. Oil sizzled in the pan. When the dumplings were finished, Andy picked one up with a fork and popped it in his mouth.

Suzy did the same. The salty-sweet dumpling tasted so delicious. "I forgot how much work it is to make these," she said.

Mum smiled. "I remember when you and Andy were younger. You'd both eat them faster than I could fry them. But it's worth it, isn't it?"

"Definitely. They're amazing," replied Suzy, smacking her lips.

Andy reached for another dumpling. "Definitely worth it."

CHAPTER 5

ONE ARM

The next day after school, Suzy marched into the gym. It buzzed with activity.

The Ravens lined up near the uneven bars and the vault. On the mat, Rebecca did a round-off followed by a back handspring, landing solidly on both feet. When she was finished, she moved over to the vault.

Suzy warmed up with a straddle stretch. The blue mat lay before her like an endless ocean. Suzy imagined herself tumbling and dancing across the mat with leaps and jumps. She liked the challenge of being graceful and powerful at the same time. For now, she would practise her routine without the tumbling passes.

Suzy pushed play on her phone and Beethoven's Fifth Symphony started.

Standing, chin up, she felt strange on the mat and clumsy with the brace on. She lifted one heel, her left arm sweeping upwards in a curve. Her hips moved in time with the chords. She did a switch leap, changing legs.

Following with a straddle jump, she pushed herself high off the mat, her legs out to the sides, toes pointed. She landed and spun around on one foot, flowing gracefully from one dance move to the next.

Stepping forward, Suzy attempted a cartwheel with one arm, but something felt not right. She wobbled, and the room spun as she landed on her bottom. She looked around, hoping nobody had witnessed her clumsy move.

Katie strutted past. "Doing okay? I'd take it easy if I were you."

Suzy's jaw tightened. She couldn't tell if Katie was being nice or making fun of her.

Across the gym, Rebecca flew through the air, her body doing a double twist off the vault before landing.

"Nice work. Do it again," said Coach.

Hopefully Coach Pat was looking the other way when I fell, thought Suzy. She felt a little envious of Coach's praise for Rebecca.

Suzy headed to the other side of the gym, where Mina performed on the balance beam. From what Suzy could tell so far, she was the chatty one on the team.

Raising both arms to her ears, Mina lunged forwards. Then, with both hands on the beam, she raised one leg, then the other. She moved her legs towards the ceiling until she was in a perfect handstand.

After holding it for several seconds, she stood upright. Then she spun around and cartwheeled forward. Finally she flipped backwards into a somersault and landed with both feet planted on the mat. She followed with a big smile.

"Now if I can just repeat this on competition day," said Mina. She pointed at the beam. "It's all yours."

Suzy mounted the beam, then walked across, toes pointed, one arm extended to steady herself. She paused, aware of the wrist brace hugging her left hand.

Stay focused. Don't fall, she thought. Coach Pat approached, and Suzy wobbled.

"How's it going?" said Coach Pat. "Wrist feeling better?"

Suzy nodded and nearly lost her balance. She hopped off the beam. "I'll be ready, Coach," she said confidently.

"Yeah. That's what I want to talk to you about." Coach sighed. "I think we should limit you to the floor routine for the upcoming meet. You'll sit out the rest of the events just this once."

"What?" replied Suzy. Her heart sank. "But Coach, I'm going to be fine."

"I think it's best for you and the team. That way you can really perfect your floor skills while you're recovering."

"But Coach –" said Suzy.

"Go and heal and focus on that floor routine," said Coach as she walked away.

Suzy nodded as she fought back tears. Floor was her best event, but she had never been limited to only one event before.

After practice, Suzy changed quickly. When she left the locker room, she saw Katie and Rebecca walking away from her down the corridor, their ponytails bouncing. Suzy followed quietly behind them.

"Can you believe it?" said Katie. "She's ruined our chances against South High."

Suzy's stomach dropped. *Are they talking about me?* she wondered.

"I know," replied Rebecca. "What awful timing."

Katie nodded. "She needs to make up for Dana, queen of the floor exercise. Shame Dana's left."

"Suzy was really stepping it up," said Rebecca. "Being new and all that."

"Yeah, but with a sprained wrist she's not going to be any help," said Katie.

Suzy stopped. Her heart pounded against her chest.

"But Coach said –" Rebecca started.

"Coach is hallucinating," said Katie. "There's no way she's going to be better before the meet against South."

"You're right," said Rebecca. "We don't stand a chance against the Panthers."

Suzy's wrist twitched. She wanted to pretend she hadn't heard what they had said.

Dashing into the nearest toilet, she waited until

the voices faded in the distance. She couldn't help but let the tears fall.

CHAPTER 6

CAGED BIRD

A couple of days passed, and Suzy had started to feel trapped, like a bird in a cage with a broken wing. She wanted to fly and feel her body twisting in the air. She kept repeating Katie and Rebecca's words in her head. *There's no way she's going to be better before the meet against South. We don't stand a chance against the Panthers.*

It was day four since she'd injured her wrist, so before practice in the locker room, Suzy removed the brace. The swelling had gone down. She slowly flexed her wrist. It felt stiff, but there was no pain. She put the brace back on. She wasn't quite ready to practise without it.

Suzy marched into the gym, and a wave of frustration took over. Her heart skipped a beat. She would show her teammates. *I'll try a one-arm handstand,* she thought. Standing on the mat, she took a deep breath.

Mina approached. "Need a spotter?" she asked Suzy. "Looks like you're going for a one-arm handstand."

"How could you tell?" asked Suzy.

Mina laughed. "I've had an injury or two. I know the routine. Shame that happened. Just before our first big meet."

"Yeah, it's not fun," replied Suzy.

"Let's do this," said Mina.

Reaching one arm above her head, Suzy stepped out with her right leg and lunged forwards. With Mina's help, she braced her right arm on the ground and lifted her back leg. Slowly, she lifted her other leg and pointed her toes.

"You've got this," said Mina. "Hold it. One, two, three, four . . ."

Suzy's arm shook, but she felt strong. She landed back on her feet and struck a finishing pose, one arm raised to her ear.

"Nice work," said Mina. "Keep going."

Mina turned and bolted down the mat. She flipped through the air a couple of times, her feet bouncing off the mat. Then she launched into a half twist before landing on both feet, her arms stretched high as she smiled.

Suzy gave Mina a thumbs-up. She felt envious. Everyone looked so good, and they were sticking their landings. They were strong and ready. Unlike her.

At least she could still do a few tumbling moves like the front tuck. She ran forwards, swinging her arms. Launching off the mat, she tucked herself in a ball, rotating forwards. She landed on her feet, taking a small step backwards. She felt a slight tweak in her wrist, but there was no pain. The brace felt snug against her hand. She had to get better and show everyone she could still perform.

* * *

At home, the house was quieter than usual. Andy was at a friend's house, and her mother would be coming home soon from work. Suzy took off the brace and pulled out the instructions from Dr Wong. She held each stretch, following the detailed instructions and doing a few extra repetitions.

Uncomfortable with the silence, Suzy moved to the living room. The oak piano stood, waiting to be played.

The doctor said she could practise in one week, depending on how she felt. It hadn't been a week yet, but Suzy's wrist definitely felt better. Playing just one song wouldn't hurt. In a way, she missed playing the piano. She often found it relaxing, and she liked her recital piece.

Sheet music lay scattered on the floor and on the bench. Suzy ran her fingers across the piano keys. She sat for a moment and started to play her recital piece – "Für Elise". She stopped playing and moved her wrist back and forth. Then she continued to play, the notes carrying her worries away.

As she finished the song, she tried to play Beethoven's Fifth Symphony just for fun. She imagined herself performing her floor routine. As the music paused, she transitioned with a toe turn. She darted down the floor at full speed and flew through the air with a front handspring. Her body rotated 360 degrees. She followed with a one-and-a-half twist, her body whipping through the air. The crowd cheered.

Just then, her mum walked in. "That sounds wonderful," she said. "Your wrist must be feeling better. I haven't heard you play for a while."

"I thought I'd give it a try," said Suzy. She thought about practice and started to hear Katie and Rebecca's voices again. Her chest grew heavy.

"You seem upset. Is something wrong?" Mum said. She was like a detective, always searching for those hidden emotions.

Suzy wanted to tell her mum about the conversation she'd overheard between Katie and Rebecca the other day, but the words were still too raw. Besides, her mum didn't want her doing gymnastics anyway.

"I'm just tired, and practice was really hard," replied Suzy.

"You practised?" Mum asked, her voice tense. "What about your wrist?"

"Coach wants me to stay in shape, so I practised with one arm," Suzy replied.

"I hope you were careful," said Mum. She stared at Suzy as if she were under a microscope. "You sure you're okay?"

"Yeah." Suzy hesitated, then took a breath and said, "But I know you don't like that I'm still doing gymnastics."

Mum sat down next to Suzy and rubbed her shoulder. "It's not that."

Suzy looked her mum in the eyes. "You never come to watch."

"Gymnastics takes up a lot of your time," Mum said. "I just want you to find a balance. Make sure you make time for other things."

"The team's counting on me," Suzy said. "Plus I love gymnastics. I have to put in a lot of work if I want to do well at the senior level."

"Well, you also have the piano recital coming up," replied Mum. "I don't want you to let that slip."

"I don't want to think about that right now," Suzy said. "The recital isn't until a week after the competition. I just want to focus on gymnastics for now."

"That's ridiculous," said Mum, frowning. "You

need to make time for your piano."

"No, I can't and I won't!" Suzy shouted. "Maybe I'll quit the recital."

"Stop being so dramatic," said Mum.

"I'm not. You just don't understand," Suzy snapped.

"I do, but it's important you make time for other things as well," said Mum.

Suzy sighed. Convincing her mum she was doing the right thing was tougher than doing a back layout off the beam.

CHAPTER 7

BUBBLE TEA

For the next several days, Suzy did her stretches and practised as hard as she could with one arm. She visualised her routines and concentrated on her floor moves, trying not to think about what Katie and Rebecca had said.

It had been almost a week since her injury, and soon she'd be able to start practising properly.

On Friday after practice, she met Tiffany at the bubble tea shop.

Taro bubble tea was Suzy's favourite. The sweet

purple drink made everything better, for a little while at least.

"How's book club?" asked Suzy, taking a sip of the bubble tea.

"It's okay," said Tiffany. "Nobody's showed up except for me and a guy who doesn't like to talk."

"That's a shame," said Suzy, staring at the painting of the panda on the wall. It was leaning against a bamboo tree, as if it didn't have a care in the world.

"Yeah, but the novel we're reading is super cool," said Tiffany. "It's going to be turned into a film. I just know it."

Suzy squinted. "Did you get your hair cut?" she asked.

"Yeah, like a week ago." Tiffany rolled her eyes and flipped her hair over her shoulder.

"Guess I've been so busy lately, I didn't notice," said Suzy.

Tiffany stirred the bubble tea with her bright-pink straw. "What did you think of the pop quiz in English?" she asked. "Yikes."

"Not good," said Suzy. "I'm pretty sure I've failed. Don't remind me. With practice every day, I haven't had time for anything else lately." Suzy took a sip of the bubble tea, swallowing her disappointment in one big gulp.

"How's your wrist?" asked Tiffany.

"Mostly better," Suzy said with a half-hearted smile.

"Really? You don't look too happy about it," said Tiffany.

Suzy sighed. "It's not because of my injury," she said. "It's just . . ."

"What?" whispered Tiffany. She leaned towards Suzy.

"After practice, I overheard Katie and Rebecca talking about me," Suzy said. "They said I've ruined our chances against South High next week. They think there's no way I'm going to be better before the meet."

Tiffany puffed out her cheeks and blew out air. "That sucks. They're your teammates. They should support you!"

Suzy shook her head, feeling a lump in her throat. She brushed away a few tears. "I feel all this pressure," she said. "I don't know if I belong on the senior team. All the older girls are super competitive."

Tiffany laughed. "And you're *not* competitive? You were killing it at your old club."

"Not any more," replied Suzy. "This injury makes everything worse. I'm scared I won't be able to perform."

"Once you're better, you'll be great!" said Tiffany.

"Yeah, I hope so." Suzy held up the bubble tea and stared into it.

"Everything's going to be fine," Tiffany said. "There's a reason you're part of the team. You have to believe in yourself."

"You're the best," said Suzy.

"That's what friends are for." Tiffany smiled.

* * *

That evening, Suzy couldn't sleep. She tossed and turned. The room felt stuffy and she couldn't breathe. She opened the window and peered outside. The stars were tiny dots of light.

Maybe I just need some fresh air, she thought. She went outside into the garden. The dewy grass tickled her toes.

Closing her eyes, she imagined herself on the mat. Beethoven's Fifth Symphony played as Suzy danced to the music. She scissor-kicked in the air and followed it up with a straddle jump. She paused, raising one arm in the air and dropping the other to her hip.

She heard the sliding glass door open from the house, and the back porch light turned on. It was

Andy.

"What are you doing out there?" he shouted.

"None of your business," said Suzy.

Andy stood on the back porch, squinting into the darkness.

"Get out of here," said Suzy.

"Are you *practising*?" he asked. "You're nuts."

"Go away," replied Suzy. "You should be sleeping."

"And you should be too. Maybe save those moves for the gym." Andy laughed.

Crickets chirped in the tall grass.

"I couldn't sleep," said Suzy. She hopped onto the brick ledge that ran along the top of the patio. "Watch this."

She jumped high in the air, holding her knees to her chest in a tight ball. She somersaulted through the air and landed, chest forward, feet together, arms out and up.

"You killed it," said Andy.

Suzy felt a sliver of hope. She'd show everyone. In just a couple of days, she would be ready to practise without the brace. She couldn't wait.

CHAPTER 8

HEALING

Monday was Suzy's first day of practice without the wrist brace. Standing by the balance beam, she stretched her arms, shoulders and neck. She slowly flexed her wrist. It felt stiff, but there was no pain.

Take it easy, she remembered Dr Wong saying. Obviously Dr Wong knew nothing about gymnastics, because there was no taking it easy.

Suzy knew she should be practising her floor routine instead, but she missed the challenge of practising other events. What if she had forgotten how to perform on the beam?

She mounted the beam and straddled it. Swinging her legs back, she crouched onto the beam, then stood up. Following with a split leap, she propelled forward from one foot, her body shaking. After she landed, she paused and prepared for a backwards walkover. She shook her left wrist side to side to get the blood flowing. Standing tall, she pulled her arms back and out. She raised her right leg, toes pointed. Then she leaned back into a back bend, keeping her eyes on the beam.

Suzy pushed off with her left leg and kicked all the way over into standing position. She felt a tug in her wrist, but moved through it.

"What are you doing, Suzy?" yelled Coach as she marched across the gym floor.

Suzy felt a knot in her stomach.

"You're supposed to be focusing on your floor routine," Coach said as she drew closer.

"Sorry, Coach. I forgot," Suzy lied, feeling a twinge of guilt.

"You need to calm down and focus on the floor," said Coach Pat as she walked away.

"Stick to your floor routine," whispered Suzy to herself. She took a sip from her water bottle and turned, her gaze moving to Rebecca on the uneven bars. Rebecca was performing a giant, rotating 360 degrees in a full extended position.

Coach Pat was now standing at Rebecca's side, arms crossed. "Remember to straighten your legs," Coach said.

Suzy felt a pang of jealousy. She wanted Coach Pat to give her advice too. It seemed like all Coach did was shout at her.

Rebecca continued to rotate around the bar three times. She finished with a double backflip off the bar. Suzy watched Rebecca's feet hit the mat. She struck her finishing pose, arms up and out.

Of course she nailed the landing, Suzy thought.

Suzy headed towards the mat. She needed to focus, but her mind raced with thoughts. The competition was creeping closer – just a week away. At least she no longer had the wrist brace. She should be happy. But what if her wrist injury had caused her to lose strength or skill?

Suzy did a few dance moves, leaping in the air and pivoting on her toes. She swayed her hips side to side, one hand in the air. Suzy took a moment and tried to clear her head, preparing for a tumbling pass. It would be the first one since her injury.

Charging onto the mat, she did a round-off, landing with both feet on the ground. She meant to follow up with a front handspring, but the thought of putting more pressure on her left wrist stopped her. She took a breath, beads of sweat dribbling down her temples.

What a wimp, she thought. *Show them you can do this.* She gave it another try, pushing through her shoulders and twisting her hips. She landed, then bounced off the mat with her toes, moving to a front handspring. She felt off-balance and awkward, but she rotated 360 degrees from her feet to hands until she fell hard onto the mat.

Suzy got up and walked away. She took a long drink from her water bottle. *Chill out,* she told herself. *Pretend nothing happened.*

Just then Katie pranced by, her blue leotard shimmering. "Coming back from an injury isn't easy," she said. "It'll get better. Hang in there."

Suzy nodded and looked away. She could feel the tears rising. The walls of the gym turned wavy like water. Across the gym, Rebecca was trying a new move off the vault. Suzy watched Rebecca push off the vault with her hands, her body twisting in the air.

Something in Suzy snapped. *A new trick! That's what you need to do,* she thought, wiping away a tear. She charged down the mat and went straight into a round-off. Her feet sprung off the mat, and instead of a half twist, she decided to do a full twist. She spun in the air, but something felt not right. She felt her legs split apart, and she barely landed on her feet and stumbled backwards.

Suzy shook her head in frustration. She waggled her wrist.

"Suzy!" Coach Pat yelled.

Great. Coach doesn't sound too happy, thought Suzy. She turned around and saw Coach Pat wave her over to the side of the gym.

As Suzy approached, she saw Coach Pat frown. "Remember to push through your shoulders," Coach said. She paused. "And what's with the full twist? Are you doing that for the meet?"

"I was thinking about it," said Suzy.

"Not a good idea," replied Coach Pat. "Stick to your routine. No new tricks. Got it?"

"Got it," said Suzy. Coach was probably right. It was a risky move coming off an injury, and Suzy knew it. But part of the thrill of gymnastics was

trying new tricks. She took a drink from her water
bottle, tempted by the idea.

* * *

For the rest of the week, Suzy practised harder
and harder. Slowly, she gained more confidence
on her tumbling passes. She performed a front
handspring, followed by a back handspring, letting
go of the tension in her wrist. Pretty soon, her body
felt lighter and she tried to forget she had injured
her wrist in the first place.

On the night before the big competition, Suzy's
mind kept replaying each move of her floor routine.
Tricks raced in her head. She was performing a full
twist off the mat, her body spiralling through the air.
As she landed, she felt a sharp pain shoot through
her left wrist and up her arm. She lost her balance
and the mat cracked open into a bottomless pit, her
body falling into a dark void.

Suzy screamed and sat upright. Her heart fluttered. "It was just a dream," she told herself. "An awful dream."

CHAPTER 9

BIG MEET

Saturday arrived, the day of the big competition. The ongoing rivalry between the North Ravens and the South Panthers was going to bring out a big crowd. The pressure was on.

Suzy sat at her kitchen table stirring the thick rice porridge in her bowl. Her stomach ached. She was too nervous to eat. She added a heaped spoonful of dried shredded pork but still couldn't bring herself to take a bite of the porridge.

She did her wrist stretches instead, moving her

wrist back and forth in a hand-shaking motion. It felt stiff but didn't hurt.

Suzy went to her room and put on the new team leotard. It was bright blue with green stripes along the sides.

At least she *looked* like a member of the team, even if she couldn't compete as well as she wanted. She glanced at her phone.

Mina would be coming in ten minutes to pick her up. She had offered to drive Suzy to the meet, since her mum wouldn't be able to. Mum had to work. Hmm. She always had an excuse when it came to the gymnastics meets. *Plus,* Suzy thought, *she's probably still upset that I'm not practising for the piano recital.*

Suzy got her kit together. Mina pulled up outside the house a few minutes later. She smiled as Suzy hopped into the car. Music played on the radio. Sweet wrappers and crumpled tissues lined the floor.

"Thanks for picking me up," said Suzy.

"No problem!" said Mina. She gave Suzy a quick

glance over. "You look like a true Raven now. I love our new uniforms. Don't you?"

"Yeah, they're super cool," said Suzy.

"And you need one of these." Mina tossed Suzy a matching green scrunchie. "I'm so freaked out about this meet. It's a big one," she said. "We've been rivals with the Panthers forever. We need to get fired up."

"Yeah," said Suzy as she fastened the scrunchie to her ponytail.

"I'm so glad you joined the team. You're going to nail your floor routine," said Mina.

"I wish everyone else felt the same way," mumbled Suzy.

"What do you mean?" asked Mina.

"Last week I overheard Katie and Rebecca talking after practice," said Suzy. "They said I've ruined our chances against South High, and there's no way I'd be better before the meet."

"You're kidding," said Mina. "That's not very nice. We're all teammates. You're so much better and you've been working really hard. Don't think about it any more."

Suzy nodded, but she felt her chest tighten. She didn't know if she could live up to all the expectations.

Mina turned off the radio. "South's gym is far bigger than ours," she said as she pulled into South High's parking lot. "Don't let it throw you off. We're a smaller school, but we have power."

Grasping her gym bag, Suzy got out of the car and followed Mina to the gym.

Mina hadn't been kidding. The Panthers' gym was huge, and the fluorescent lights were almost blinding.

The Panthers were on the opposite side of the gym. Their bright orange and black leotards shimmered in the light. The Panthers had their game faces on. They were ready to dominate. Suzy could see it in their eyes.

Suzy stretched with her team. She felt the energy

in the air. The North High Ravens were pumped too. And they were depending on her.

"Is your wrist OK?" asked Rebecca. "You're going to kill it." The green stripes on her leotard gleamed.

That's weird, thought Suzy. *I know what you really think about me.*

Suzy gave a thumbs-up anyway. She tried to forget what she had overheard Rebecca and Katie saying last week, but the words were seared in her brain.

She's ruined our chances against South High. What awful timing.

After stretching, Suzy went through a few dance moves on the mat. She imagined Beethoven's Fifth Symphony playing in the background. Then she started to think about the piano recital and her mum.

A heaviness settled in her chest, and Suzy felt as if she were moving in slow motion. She took a long, leaping step and tried to launch off the floor with her feet. Her body took flight, and she scissor-kicked her legs into a split in mid-air.

She landed back on the mat and stopped. Her breath quickened and she leaned forward, resting her hands on her knees and breathing deeply.

That felt a lot harder than it should have, Suzy thought.

Mina walked over, her ponytail bobbing. "You okay?" she asked.

Suzy swallowed. "I feel like a sloth. Slow and heavy."

"Stay strong," said Mina. "Be in your body. Don't think too much."

Mina headed to the opposite side of the gym to the vault. She hurdled onto the springboard and did a front handspring onto the table. She followed with a front tuck, her body somersaulting through the air, dark ponytail whipping around. She landed and stretched her arms up in a finishing pose, smiling ear to ear.

Coach Pat gave Mina an approving nod.

Suzy wished Coach would be proud of her too.

Believe in yourself, Suzy told herself.

She closed her eyes and imagined herself running full speed down the mat. She bounced off her feet and moved into a front tuck followed by a round-off and a back layout.

Coach Pat jogged over from the other side of the gym. "Hey, Suzy! You've got this."

"Thanks, Coach," Suzy replied, taking a deep breath.

After warm-ups, the team waited for the meet to start. Suzy glanced up into the stands. She searched the crowd, hoping by chance her mum had changed her mind. She wanted to surprise her with the music she picked. But there was no sign of her mum anywhere.

CHAPTER 10

ANOTHER CHANCE

The teams lined up and marched in with their gymnast walk – straight arms, straight legs, hands graceful at their sides. The Ravens were first on the vault.

Mina saluted the judge then found her spot by the tape. She sprinted towards the vault, arms pumping. Flying off the springboard, she pushed off the vault with her hands, her feet flying overhead. Her body twisted in the air just before sticking the landing. The crowd cheered.

Suzy stood and clapped for Mina. Her stomach growled and she felt light-headed.

She should have eaten breakfast.

Katie was last on the vault.

"Go, girl!" Suzy yelled. The least she could do was support the team, even though she had a hard time forgetting what Katie had said about her.

Katie exploded off the springboard and pushed off the table with both hands, her body flipping upside down.

She moved into a full twist, her body spinning through the air. She nailed the landing and finished her pose with a big smile. The crowd roared.

Suzy wanted to be happy for Katie and the team, but fear gripped her. She didn't want to mess up her floor routine. Not when everything was going so well for the Ravens. She moved her wrist back and forth.

Maybe she needed something to eat.

At the snack bar, Suzy bought a granola bar and a banana.

A familiar voice came from behind her. "Good idea. I noticed you didn't touch the rice porridge this morning."

Suzy spun around. "Mum? What are you doing here?" she asked.

Andy and Tiffany popped forward from behind Mum and smiled.

"And you guys too?" Suzy asked, beaming.

Mum gave Suzy's shoulder a squeeze. "I know you have been so busy, but you've worked hard and you're brave," she said. "Even after your injury, you kept pushing through. I'm proud of you. Plus, someone convinced me that I had better not miss this meet or I'd be sorry." Mum turned and winked at Tiffany.

"I'll practise piano after this meet," said Suzy. "I promise. I'm just so nervous for my floor routine."

"You can do this," Mum said. She opened her arms, and Suzy found herself in a warm embrace. "Just try your best out there. That's all you can ever do."

"I'm so glad you're here," said Suzy.

"We'll be rooting for you," said Tiffany, grinning.

"You're going to smash it," added Andy.

Tiffany and Andy each gave Suzy a high five.

Suzy took a quick bite of the granola bar and walked back into the gym, her head held high. She felt a sudden burst of energy. She was ready to give it her all.

Suzy sat down with the team and watched a South High Panther on the uneven bars. The opponent soared through the air, her shiny orange leotard reflecting the bright lights. She circled the bar three times, her legs splaying out, then together, toes pointed. Then she released the bar, and her body flipped twice in mid-air before landing on the mat. She looked flawless.

The competition was close. The Ravens performed well on the bars and beam. They were up by several points. The floor exercise would be their last event.

Suzy's mind spun. She tried to remember what her mum had said. *Try your best. That's all you can ever do.* Suzy had prepared the best she could, even with the injury. Maybe she'd even add a twist to her routine. She could do this!

"You're up next, Suzy," said Coach Pat.

Suzy took off her warm-up jacket and marched onto the mat. The judge signalled, and Suzy saluted back and smiled.

The music started and she stood tall with her arms at her sides. Her mum would be surprised with the music she chose. Suzy swung her hips to the left, then to the right, and danced across the mat. She tuned out everything around her.

She paused, preparing for her first tumbling pass. Then she dashed forwards, arms pumping. Her feet bounced off the mat as she cartwheeled through the air. Her body flipped forwards and her feet bounced off the mat. Then she flipped backwards. She landed, taking a tiny step forward. Suzy quickly moved to a dance step. Then she took a leap followed by a scissor kick in the air. She pirouetted on her toes.

On her last pass, Suzy hurtled forwards into a round-off, her feet swinging over her head. She pushed through her toes then arched backwards, hands then feet punching off the mat. She felt a slight tug in her wrist, but her body twisted in the air as she flipped upside down into a full twist, body extended. She stuck the landing, feet planted on the mat. Her hands shot up and out in a finishing pose.

After her routine, loud cheers erupted from the stands. Suzy spotted Mum, Andy and Tiffany. All three were standing and clapping. Her mum had a big smile. It almost looked as if she was crying at the same time. Suzy's wrist throbbed, but she had made it through. She felt proud.

Coach Pat and the team crowded around Suzy with hugs and high fives.

"Nice work." Coach Pat winked. "You nailed it."

"Way to rock," said Mina. "We've definitely won

this now."

"You did it," added Rebecca.

Katie pulled Suzy close. "Sorry about what we said. Mina told us you overheard our conversation about you. We were wrong." Katie gave Suzy a big hug. "We're lucky to have you on the team."

"I'm grateful to be part of this team," replied Suzy, feeling the tension melt away. She looked at all her teammates and smiled. Their matching bright-blue leotards shimmered like stars.

ABOUT the AUTHOR

Selina Li Bi enjoys creating characters who live in magical and multicultural worlds. She has an MFA degree in creative writing and practised as an optometrist for many years. An exercise enthusiast, she enjoys running and yoga. She now lives in Fargo, North Dakota, USA, with her family and two furry writing companions.

GLOSSARY

alignment being in a straight line

brace object fastened to something else to provide support

clumsy careless and awkward in your movements

comeback return to a former position

dramatic expressing more feeling than is necessary

fluorescent giving out a bright light by using a certain type of energy

hallucinate hear or see things that are not really there

repetition the act of repeating something

routine series of tricks linked one after another in a performance

sprain injure a joint by twisting or tearing its muscles or ligaments

visualise see something in your mind

DISCUSSION QUESTIONS

1. What characteristics does Suzy have that are different from her mum? Discuss using examples from the text.

2. Suzy faces a challenge when she injures her wrist. Have you faced a challenge in a sport or hobby? Talk about how your experience was similar or different.

3. In addition to her love for gymnastics, Suzy also likes playing the piano. What are two of your favourite activities? Do you ever have trouble balancing them?

WRITING PROMPTS

1. Explain the main problem Suzy faces in the book. Then write a letter to Suzy giving her advice on how to handle this problem.

2. In Chapter 5, Suzy overhears a couple of her teammates talking about her. How do you think the scene would've been different if she'd confronted them about it? Write a version of the scene where this happens.

3. Tiffany, Suzy's best friend, offers her support in this story. Write about a time when a friend supported you. How did your friend show his or her support?

MORE ABOUT FLOOR EXERCISE

The floor mat, where the floor exercise takes place, is a square about 12 metres wide by 12 metres long. It sometimes has springs underneath it to help propel tumbling moves.

For female gymnasts, floor routines are usually performed to music and incorporate dance moves.

At Olympic level, gymnasts typically try to include four or five tumbling passes during a floor routine.

Athletes can lose points during the floor routine by stepping out of bounds or going over the 90-second time limit.

At the 2019 US Gymnastics Championships, gymnastics superstar Simone Biles completed a triple twisting-double somersault during her floor routine. She became the first female gymnast to complete this skill in competition. A triple-double, as it is often called, is a double backflip with three twists.

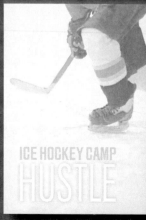
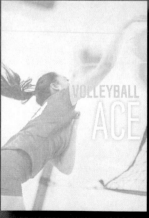